BASEBALL: OUR GAME

JOHN THORN

BASEBALL: OUR GAME

penguin books

PENGUIN BOOKS

Published by the Penguin Group
Penguin Books USA Inc., 375 Hudson Street,
New York, New York 10014, U.S.A.
Penguin Books Ltd, 27 Wrights Lane,
London W8 5TZ, England
Penguin Books Australia Ltd, Ringwood,
Victoria, Australia
Penguin Books Canada Ltd, 10 Alcorn Avenue,
Toronto, Ontario, Canada M4V 3B2
Penguin Books (N.Z.) Ltd, 182–190 Wairau Road,
Auckland 10, New Zealand

Penguin Books Ltd, Registered Offices:
Harmondsworth, Middlesex, England

Published in Penguin Books 1995

"Our Game" appears in *Total Baseball* (fourth edition) edited by John
Thorn and Pete Palmer with Michael Gershman, Viking Penguin,
1995.

ISBN 0 14 60.0111 7

Printed in the United States of America

CONTENTS

Baseball has been, most often for better but occasionally for worse, the American game. It has given our people rest and recreation, myths and memories, heroes and history and hope. It has mirrored our society, sometimes propelling it with models for democracy, community, commerce, and common humanity, sometimes lagging behind with equally instructive models of futility and resistance to change. And as our national game, baseball in no small measure defines us as Americans, connecting us with our countrymen across all barriers of generation, class, race, and creed.

Baseball in the Americas is more than a game. It is first and foremost about play, a fact obscured amid today's ferment of free agency, salary caps, and threatened cataclysm. Some 150 years ago, an overly solemn America was first indebted to baseball for the freedom it gave to play. Let's look at how child's play came to be our national pastime.

America Learns to Play

Even when baseball was in its infancy in the 1850s—
having just evolved from the boyhood game of rounders
and its more formalized derivative, town ball—the sport
was already shaping the life of the country. Americans of
the previous generation had been blind to the virtue of
play, much perplexing our European cousins. We permitted ourselves few amusements that could not be justified
in terms of social or business utility, or "seriousness."
Nonconformists like the Olympic Town Ball Club of
Philadelphia in the 1830s had to put up with a lot of guff,
as this contemporary account details:

> The first day that the Philadelphia men took the field
> . . . only four men were found to play, so they started in
> by playing a game called cat ball. All the players were
> over twenty-five years of age, and to see them playing a
> game like this caused much merriment among the

friends of the players. It required "sand" in those days to go out on the field and play, as the prejudice against the game was very great. It took nearly a whole season to get men enough together to make a team, owing to the ridicule heaped upon the players for taking part in such childish sports.

What brought scorn upon the heads of these staunch devotees of town ball (also known as "Boston Ball" or the "Massachusetts Game") was that although the game had regularly positioned fielders and demanded a modicum of strategic play, it still bore the childish essence of rounders: the retirement of a baserunner by throwing the ball *at* him, which necessitated a softer, less resilient ball than that used in the manly sport of cricket. Who was the genius who came up with the idea of retiring a runner by touching him with the ball or securing it "in the hands of an adversary on the base"? Perhaps it was Alexander Cartwright, who is known to many as "the man who invented baseball," though baseball was not invented; it evolved. But it may have been Daniel Lucius Adams or William Wheaton or Lewis F. Wadsworth.

No matter—this was the first step toward making an

American game that could challenge boys and men alike, and that could take its place in the life of our nation as cricket had done in England. Henry Chadwick, the English-born cricket reporter who coined the term "national pastime" and became known as the "Father of Baseball," wrote that early on he

... was struck with the idea that base ball was just the game for a national sport for Americans and ... that from this game of ball a powerful lever might be made by which our people could be lifted into a position of more devotion to physical exercise and healthful outdoor recreation than they had, hitherto, been noted for.... In fact, as is well-known, we were the regular target for the shafts of raillery and even abuse from our outdoor-sport-loving cousins of England, in consequence of our national neglect of sports and pastimes, and our too great devotion to business and the "Almighty Dollar." But thanks to Base Ball ... we have been transformed into quite another people....

The transformation was from a hard-working but grim citizenry to a nation devoted to fresh air and exercise, not unlike the current rage for jogging, aerobics, and body building. Amateur baseball clubs sprang up like dandelions in the years immediately before the Civil War, but these were formed more for camaraderie and calisthenics than the pursuit of victory or the honing of skills. The demands of the new game on athleticism were few, as the one-bound rule remained in effect (an out was recorded if a ball was caught on a bounce), and a couple of weeks' practice were enough to make a novice of forty a creditable player. Men viewed baseball as a mild pastime, or relief from the mental strains of work; as a tonic, restorative of the physical energies needed for work; or as a release of the surplus nervous energy that impedes young men in their pursuit of purposeful work. America in the mid-1850s was learning how to play, but still viewed sport in terms of its salutary effects on commerce; not until the close of the War Between the States would the focus shift to learning how to play well—for its own sake.

The Charm of the Game

Today we think of baseball as an anachronism, a last vestige of America's agrarian paradise—an idyllic game that takes us back to a more innocent time. But baseball originated in New York City, not rural Cooperstown, and in truth it was an exercise in nostalgia from the beginning. Alexander Cartwright and his Knickerbockers began play in Madison Square in 1842, and the city's northward progress soon compelled them to move uptown to Murray Hill. When the grounds there were also threatened by the march of industry, the Knicks ferried across the Hudson River to the Elysian Fields of Hoboken, a landscaped retreat of picnic ground and scenic vistas that was designed by its proprietors to relieve New Yorkers of city air and city care. In other words, the purpose of baseball's primal park was the same as that of New York's Central Park or, much later, Boston's Fenway Park—to give an increasingly urban populace a park within the city, a place reminiscent of the idealized farms that had sent all these lads to the metropolis.

Thus the attraction of the game in its earliest days was first the novelty and exhilaration of play; second the opportunity for deskbound city clerks to expend surplus energy in a sylvan setting, freed from the tyranny of the clock; and third, to harmonize with an American golden age that was almost entirely legendary.

Simple charms, simple pleasures. In the late 1860s, advancing skills led to heightened appetites for victory, which led to hot pursuit of the game's gifted players, which inevitably led to *sub rosa* payments and, by 1870, rampant professionalism. (Doesn't that chain reaction put one in mind of college football or basketball?) The gentlemanly players of baseball's first generation retreated from the field, shaking their heads in dismay at how greed had perverted the "grand old game"—now barely twenty years old—and probably ruined it forever.

Sound familiar? It should—the same dire and premature announcements of the demise of the game have been issued ever since, spurred by free-agent signings, long-term contracts, no-trade provisions, strikes and lockouts, integration, night ball, rival leagues, ad infinitum. The only conclusions a calm head might draw from this recurring cycle of disdain for the present and glorification of the past are that (a) things aren't what they used to be and never were; (b) accurate assessment of a present predicament is impossible, for it requires perspective; and (c) no matter what the owners or players or rulesmakers or fans do, they can't kill baseball. All three conclusions are correct. In baseball, the distinction between amateur and professional is not clear-cut: an amateur may play for devotion to the game (*amat* being the Latin for love), but a professional does not play for pursuit of gain alone; he plays for love, too.

Oh, don't you remember the game of base-ball we saw
    twenty years ago played,
When contests were true, and the sight free to all, and
    home-runs in plenty were made?
When we lay on the grass, and with thrills of delight,
    watched the ball squarely pitched at the bat,
And easily hit, and then mount out of sight along with
    our cheers and our hat?
And then, while the fielders raced after the ball, the
    men on the bases flew round,

And came in together—four batters in all. Ah! That was
the old game renowned.
Now salaried pitchers, who throw the ball curved at
padded and masked catchers lame
And gate-money music and seats all reserved is all that
is left of the game.
Oh, give us the glorious matches of old, when love of
true sport made them great,
And not this new-fashioned affair always sold for the
boodle they take at the gate.

H.C. Dodge

That doomsday ditty was published in 1886.

The National Pastime

America before the Civil War was still populated by a handful of veterans of the Revolutionary War and many who remembered vividly the War of 1812. The era of Anglo–American amity had not yet dawned; our country's spiritual separation from the Mother Country, though effected by treaty in 1783, was still in process. And having baseball to rival and replace cricket was an important step in that process. Moreover when England, seeking to maintain its supply of cotton from the American South, appeared over-cordial to the Confederate cause, anti-British feeling swept the North. An American long suffering from an inferiority complex toward England now turned against cricket and embraced baseball with increased fervor.

From 1856 on, Henry Chadwick had been eager for baseball to rise to the status in America that cricket held in his native England. He championed the game tirelessly, helping to refine its rules and practices to make it the equal of cricket as a "manly" and "scientific" game. And baseball soon became, in his words, like cricket "a game requiring the mental powers of judgment, calculation and quick perception to excel in it—while in its demands upon the vigor, endurance and courage of manhood, its requirements excel those requisite to become equally expert as a cricketer."

Chadwick invented a method of scorekeeping and statistical compilation patterned on those which were inaugurated in cricket. Baseball was an elemental game— pitch, hit, catch, throw—like other games of ball; but keeping records of the contests and later printing box scores and individual averages elevated it from rounders and placed it on an equal footing with its transatlantic counterpart. (As important, the records served to legitimize men's concern with what had been merely a boys' exercise by making it more systematic, like the numerically annotated world of business.) Today a baseball without records is inconceivable: They are what keep Babe Ruth and Ty Cobb and Walter Johnson alive in our minds in a way that President James K. Polk, Walter

Reed, or Admiral Dewey—arguably greater men—are not.

By the end of the Civil War cricket in this country remained a pastime for a shrinking band of Anglophiles, while the New York Game of Baseball (as it was then called to differentiate it from the nearly vanished Massachusetts Game) was spreading across the country, courtesy of returning veterans whose first exposure to baseball might have come in a prisoner-of-war camp. In the press, baseball was typically proclaimed The National Game—the same term Britons used for cricket.

Play for Pay

From its creation in 1871 to its crash five years later, the National Association had a rocky time as America's first professional league. Franchises came and went with dizzying speed, often folding in midseason. Schedules were not played out if a club slated to go on the road saw little prospect of gain. Drinking and gambling and game-fixing were rife. And the Boston Red Stockings of Al Spalding and the Wright brothers dominated play, going 71–8 in the last of their four straight championship seasons; their predictable and one-sided victories crushed the competition and at last, interest in the entire circuit.

But from the ashes of the National Association emerged the Red Stockings' model of success and the entrepreneurial genius of Chicago's William Hulbert. After raiding Boston to obtain four of the biggest stars in the game—Spalding, Ross Barnes, Deacon White, and Cal McVey—and lining up the services of the Philadelphia Athletics' Adrian Anson, the White Stockings were ready to roll in the National League of Professional Base Ball Clubs, founded on February 2, 1876 in New York's Grand Central Hotel.

The first five years of the NL were nearly as unsettled as the final years of the NA, with franchises appearing and then disappearing in such cities as Syracuse, Indianapolis, and Hartford while major cities like New York and Philadelphia were, after the league's inaugural year, unrepresented. In 1878 the fledgling circuit was forced to cut back to six teams: Milwaukee, Indianapolis, Chicago, Providence, Cincinnati, and Boston. *National* League? *National* Game? It seemed Americans had plenty of appetite for playing the game, but not much for watching it.

Yet as the National League suffered with growing pains, it was introducing some elements that were critical to the explosion of interest that came with the 1880s. It created a professional (paid) umpiring crew; insisted that the league schedule be honored; banned pool selling and hard-liquor consumption in the stands; and created a system of management-owned teams as opposed to the player-run cooperatives that had largely characterized the

NA. As the public's renewed faith in the integrity of the game coincided with an upswing in the national economy, not only did the National League flourish; along came an interloper, the rival American Association, to offer patrons 25-cent baseball (NL admissions were 50 cents), Sunday games, and beer. With the public's new appetite for the game seeming insatiable, a group of investors led by St. Louis' Henry Lucas launched a *third* major league, the Union Association, for 1884.

As brash stars like Cap Anson, Tim Keefe, Dan Brouthers, and the larger-than-life King Kelly captured the newspaper headlines and the nation's imagination, the age of the baseball idol arrived. Before this decade, men like Jim Creighton, Joe Start, and George Wright had been admired in New York and New England, but now a baseball hero's image could be mass-produced for nationwide sale, or licensed for advertising, or inspire odes and songs. Kelly inspired "Slide, Kelly, Slide," its arcane references now largely forgotten but once the most popular song in the land:

Slide, Kelly, slide!
Your running's a disgrace!

Slide, Kelly, slide!
Stay there, hold your base!
If someone doesn't steal ya,
And your batting doesn't fail ya,
They'll take you to Australia!
Slide, Kelly, slide!

And although Ernest Lawrence Thayer always denied it, Kelly could well have been the model for "Casey at the Bat," the immortal lyric ballad Thayer penned in 1888. ("Casey" was sometimes reprinted in the newspapers of the 1880s as "Kelly at the Bat," changing the locale from Mudville to Beantown.)

Baseball was ascendant in the 1880s, and like the budding nation whose pastime it was, pretty cocksure of itself. In the same year that "Casey" made his debut, Albert Spalding led a contingent of baseball players on a round the world tour, spreading the gospel of bat and ball to such places as Egypt, Italy, England, Hawaii, and the above-mentioned Australia. Baseball, America thought, was too grand a game to be merely a national pastime; it ought to be the international pastime.

At a New York banquet for Spalding's returning

"world tourists" in 1889, speaker Mark Twain declared, "Baseball is the very symbol, the outward and visible expression of the drive and push and rush and struggle of the raging, tearing, booming nineteenth century." Spalding himself later wrote:

> I claim that Base Ball owes its prestige as our National Game to the fact that as no other form of sport it is the exponent of American Courage, Confidence, Combativeness; American Dash, Discipline, Determination; American Energy, Eagerness, Enthusiasm; American Pluck, Persistency, Performance; American Spirit, Sagacity, Success; American Vim, Vigor, Virility.

In fact baseball had become more than the mere reflection of our rising industrial and political power and its propensity for bluster and hokum: the national game was beginning to *supply* emblems for democracy, industry, and community that would change America and the world—not in the ways that Spalding's Tourists may have envisioned, but indisputably for the better.

A Model Institution

Father Chadwick had been typically prescient when he wrote in 1876, the inaugural year of the National League and the centenary of America's birth:

> What Cricket is to an Englishman, Base-Ball has become to an American.... On the Cricket-field—and there only—the Peer and the Peasant meet on equal terms; the possession of courage, nerve, judgment, skill, endurance and activity alone giving the palm of superiority. In fact, a more democratic institution does not exist in Europe than this self-same Cricket; and as regards its popularity, the records of the thousands of Commoners, Divines and Lawyers, Legislators and Artisans, and Literateurs as well as Mechanics and Laborers, show how great a hold it has on the people. If this is the characteristic of Cricket in aristocratic and monarchial England, how much more will the same characteristics mark Base-Ball in democratic and republican America.

Chadwick's vision of baseball as a model democratic institution would have to wait for the turn of the century to be fully articulated, and for Jackie Robinson and Branch Rickey to be fully realized. But Chadwick's belief that baseball could be more than a game, could become a model of and for American life, presaged baseball's golden age of 1903–30.

The tumultuous 1890s witnessed a player revolt against high-handed and monopolistic management, epitomized by a cap on salaries, followed by a nearly ruinous contraction from three major leagues to one twelve-team circuit. The national economy suffered a panic in 1893 and a sluggish recovery thereafter; baseball attendance dwindled; and the lack of postseason interleague competition after 1890 (as there had been since 1884) was sorely felt. The game was in a period of consolidation, or hibernation, or stagnation; one's perspective depended upon whether he were an owner, fan, or player.

But then Ban Johnson came along, fired by the same vision of a rival league that had inflamed the Players League and the American and Union Associations before him, and that would beckon to the Federal and Continental Leagues later on. With the declaration by the American League that it would conduct business as a major league in 1901, and the signing of a peace treaty with the Nationals two years later, the World Series was resumed, prosperity returned, and the popularity and influence of the game exploded.

Baseball mania seized America as new heroes like Christy Mathewson, Honus Wagner, Ty Cobb, Walter Johnson, and Nap Lajoie found a public hungry for knowledge of their every action, their every thought. A fan's affiliation with his team could exceed in vigor his attachment to his church, his trade, his political party— all but family and country, and even these were wrapped up in baseball. The national pastime became the great repository of national ideals, the symbol of all that was good in American life: fair play (sportsmanship); the rule of law (objective arbitration of disputes); equal opportunity (each side has its innings); the brotherhood of man (bleacher harmony); and more.

The baseball boom of the early twentieth century built on the game's simple charms of exercise and communal celebration, adding the psychological and social complexities of vicarious play: civic pride, role models, and hero worship. It became routine for the President to throw out the first ball of the season. Supreme Court Justices had inning-by-inning scores from the World Series relayed to their chambers. Business leaders, perhaps disingenuously, praised baseball as a model of competition and fair play. "Baseball," opined a writer for *American Magazine* in 1913, "has given our public a fine lesson in commercial morals. . . . Some day all business will be reorganized and conducted by baseball standards."

Leaders of recent immigrant groups advised their peoples to learn the national game if they wanted to become Americans, and foreign-language newspapers devoted space to educating their readers about America's strange and wonderful game. (New York's *Staats-Zeitung*, for example, applauded *Kraftiges Schlagen*—hard hitting—and cautioned German fans not to kill the *Unparteiischer*.) As historian Harold Seymour wrote, "The argot of baseball supplied a common means of communication and strengthened the bond which the game helped to establish among those sorely in need of it—the mass of urban dwellers and immigrants living in the anonymity and impersonal vortex of large industrial cities. . . . With the loss of the traditional ties known in a rural society, baseball gave to many the feeling of belonging." And rooting for a baseball team permitted city folk, newcomers and native-born, the sense of pride in community that in former times—when they may have lived in small towns—was commonplace.

Thus baseball offered a model of how to be an American, to be part of the team: Baseball was "second only to death as a leveler," wrote essayist Allen Sangree. Even in those horrifically leveling years of 1941–45, when so many of our bravest and best gave their lives to defend American ideals, baseball's role as a vital enterprise was confirmed by President Franklin Delano Roosevelt's "green light" for continued play. Many of baseball's finest players—Ted Williams, Joe DiMaggio, Hank Greenberg, Bob Feller, to name a few—swapped their baseball gear for Uncle Sam's, and served with military distinction or helped to boost the nation's morale. Even oldtimers like Babe Ruth, Walter Johnson, and Ty Cobb donned uniforms in service of their country—baseball uniforms, as they staged exhibitions on behalf of war bonds. Servicemen overseas looked to letters from home and the box scores in *The Sporting News* to keep them in touch with what they had left behind, and what they were fighting for—an American way of life that was a beacon for a world in which the light of freedom had been nearly extinguished.

I was one of the countless immigrants who from the 1860s on saw baseball as the "open sesame" to the door of their adopted land. A Polish Jew born in occupied Germany to Holocaust survivors, I arrived on these shores at age two. After checking in at Ellis Island, I happened by chance to spend the first night in my new land in the no-longer-elegant hotel where in 1876 the National League had been founded. I learned to read by studying the backs of Topps baseball cards, and to be an American by attaching myself passionately to the Brooklyn Dodgers (who also taught me about the fickleness of love).

The Brooklyn Dodgers, in the persons particularly of Rickey and Robinson, also taught America a lesson: that baseball's integrative and democratic models, by the 1940s long held to be verities, were hollow at the core.

David Halberstam has written:

. . . it was part of our folklore, basic to our national democratic myth, that sports was the great American equalizer, that money and social status did not matter upon the playing fields. Elsewhere life was assumed to be unfair: those who had privilege passed it on to their children, who in turn had easier, softer lives. Those without privilege were doomed to accept the essential injustices of daily life. But according to the American myth, in sports the poor but honest kid from across the tracks could gain (often in competition with richer, snottier kids) recognition and acclaim for his talents.

Until October 23, 1945, when Robinson signed a contract to play for the Montreal Royals, Brooklyn's top farm club, the myth as far as African Americans were concerned was not a sustaining legend but a mere falsehood.

Rickey's rectitude and Robinson's courage have become central parables of baseball and America, exemplars of decency and strength that inspire all of us. Their "great experiment" came too late for such heroes of black ball as Josh Gibson and Oscar Charleston and Ray Dandridge, but its success has been complete. Once the integrative or leveling model of baseball—all America playing and working in harmony—was extended to

African Americans, the effect on the nation was pro-
found. Eighty years after the Civil War, America had
proved itself unable to practice the values for which it
was fought; baseball showed the way. This is what Commissioner Ford Frick said to the St. Louis Cardinals, ru-
mored to be planning a strike in May 1947:

> If you do this you will be suspended from the league.
> You will find that the friends you think you have in the
> press box will not support you, that you will be outcasts.
> I do not care if half the league strikes. Those who do it
> will encounter quick retribution. They will be sus-
> pended and I don't care if it wrecks the National
> League for five years. This is the United States of
> America, and one citizen has as much right to play as
> any other. The National League will go down the line
> with Robinson whatever the consequence.

As Monte Irvin said, "Baseball has done more to
move America in the right direction than all the professional patriots with their billions of cheap words." The
Supreme Court decision of *Brown v Topeka Board of
Education;* civil rights heroes like Martin Luther King,

Jr., James Meredith, Thurgood Marshall, and others; the freedom marches and the voting rights act—all were vital to America's progress toward unity, but the title of one of Jackie Robinson's books may not overstate the case: *Baseball Has Done It.*

A final way in which baseball supplies models for America is one that has been present from the game's beginning: a model for children wishing to be grownups, wrestling with their insecurities and wondering, *What does it mean to be a man? What does a man do?* (Most of us old boys occasionally wonder this as well.) The answers in baseball, at least, are unequivocal; as Satchel Paige said in his later years, "I loved baseball. There wasn't no 'maybe so' about it."

Baseball gives children a sense of how wide the world is, in its possibilities but also in its geography. Reading the summations of minor-league ball in *The Sporting News* each week piqued the curiosity of baseball-mad boys like me: where were Kokomo and Mattoon and Thibodeaux and Nogales? How did people behave in Salinas or Rocky Mount? What did they eat in Artesia? How many exciting, exotic places this enormous country contained! But a note of comfort—they couldn't be all that strange if baseball was played there.

And to that other vast *terra incognita*—the world of adults—baseball also offered a road map. How many boys and girls learned to talk with adults, principally their fathers, by nodding wisely at an assessment of a shortstop's range or a pitcher's heart, and mock-confidently venturing an opinion about the hometown team's chances? Our dads are our first heroes (and, decades later, our last); but in between, baseball players are what we want to be. For heroes are larger than life, and when as adults we have taken the measure of ourselves and found we are no more than life-size, and on our bad days seemingly less than that, baseball can puff us up a bit.

Douglass Wallop put it nicely:

. . . only yesterday the fan was a kid of nine or ten bolting his breakfast on Saturday morning and hurtling from the house with a glove buttoned over his belt and a bat over his shoulder, rushing to the nearest vacant lot, perhaps the nearest alley, where the other guys were gathering, a place where it would always be spring. For him, baseball would always have the sound and look and smell of that morning and of other mornings just like it. Only by an accident of chance would he find himself, in the years to come, up in the grandstand, looking on. But for a quirk of fate, he himself would be down on that field; it would be his likeness on the television screen and his name in the newspaper high on the list of .300 hitters. He was a fan, but a fan only incidentally. He was, first and always, himself a baseball player.

The Fifties

If the America that was survives anywhere as more than a memory, it is in baseball, that strangely pastoral game in no matter what setting—domed stadium or Little League field. As hindsight improves upon foresight, memory improves upon reality, so that the endless monotony and grinding physical labor of small-town life before the Civil War are now thought quite romantic. For all our complaints today, it may likewise be argued that America is better than it ever was.

Given the calamitous labor-management war of 1994, there are few who would say the same about baseball. However, today's players *are* better than those in the game's golden age; the strategy of the game and even its execution are more adept (forget all that moaning about how nobody knows the "fundamentals" any more . . . the average player of fifty years ago didn't know them either); and the opportunities to watch baseball, if not to play it, far exceed those of say, the 1950s, today broadly regarded as the game's halcyon era. (A golden age may be defined flexibly, it seems, so as to coincide with the period of one's youth.) For all its pull toward the good old days, for all its statistical illusions of an Olympian era when titans strode the basepaths, for all its seeming permanence in a world aswirl with change, baseball has in fact moved with America, and improved with it.

The period after World War II was a heady time for the nation and its pastime, both of them buoyed by returning veterans and removed restrictions. But in 1946 the major leagues still represented only the sixteen cities that had participated in the National Agreement of 1903, none west of St. Louis; a handful of African Americans were just entering the minor leagues after a half-century's exclusion; and because television was not yet a staple of the American home, most baseball fans had never seen *even a single big-league game*.

Women had been courted as patrons (even nonpaying patrons) ever since the game's dawn. Baseball management hoped that their presence would lend "tone" to the proceedings and keep a lid on the rowdies, in the stands and on the field. But women's participation in the game's labor force and management was even more limited than their role in the nation's business and industry—Rosie the Riveter and Eleanor Roosevelt as yet had no counterparts in Organized Baseball. The All-American Girls Baseball League made its debut in 1943, the brainchild of Chicago Cubs' owner Philip K. Wrigley. The women's "league of their own" won many admirers over the next decade, but the majors always regarded it as separate and unequal.

On the amateur level, while American Legion Junior Baseball had begun as early as 1928, and Little League in 1939, neither attained their heights until after the War ended. Naysayers will point out that baseball has lost ground as more kids today play football, basketball, soccer, and tennis than fifty years ago—but far more play baseball, too, and not only in America. The annual pursuit of the Little League championship in Williamsport, Pennsylvania (like the Pan-American Games), has become an international affair, an instrument of diplomacy that State Department officials envy. Indeed, baseball may yet hold the key to neighborly relations with all nations in the hemisphere.

Baseball in the colleges, now so vibrant and so fertile

with major league talent, was on the path to extinction by the end of the War, only to be brought back from the brink by the G.I. Bill; the explosive growth in enrollment that the returning veterans produced also created a sudden need for expanded athletic programs, and baseball was the prime beneficiary. The NCAA's introduction of the College World Series in 1947 affirmed the game's recovery on campus, and since locating in Omaha three years later it has grown steadily.

In 1951 Major League Baseball, as dated from the inception of the National League in 1876, reached the august age of 75 and proclaimed its "diamond jubilee." Celebratory banquets were held, a plaque was erected at the old hotel where the league was founded, and all NL players wore a commemorative patch on their sleeves. (Coincidentally but less flashily the American League marked its fiftieth birthday as a major circuit.) Let's take a moment to look at where baseball stood at that point.

There was no question it was booming. On the professional level, a whopping 59 leagues contained 448 teams employing about 8,000 players—or 19 minor leaguers competing for each of the then 400 spots in the big show. Little League would soon send its first alumnus to the majors, which had already accepted hundreds of graduates from Legion and other programs. Happy Chandler secured from television a then mind-boggling but now quaint $6 million for broadcast rights to the next six World Series. And with the game's most powerful teams bunched in New York City—the Yankees, the Dodgers, and the Giants—the publicity mills and the turnstiles were spinning as they had never spun before.

But the excitement of the first five postwar years was not confined to New York: even such perennial tailenders as the Boston Braves, the Philadelphia Phillies, and the Cleveland Indians fought their way into the World Series; and staid old Cleveland, under Bill Veeck's carnival-barker aegis, set staggering new attendance records. Many of the newly admitted African-American players had become stars and—satisfyingly, though few but Branch Rickey had predicted it—box-office attractions: Jackie Robinson, Roy Campanella, and Don Newcombe of the Dodgers; Monte Irvin and rookie Willie Mays of the Giants; Sam Jethroe of the Braves; Larry Doby and Satchel Paige of the Indians. Many prewar stars continued to shine, like Bob Feller, Stan

Musial, and Ted Williams (though with the Korean War he answered Uncle Sam's call yet again), and new ones like Gotham's center field trio of Duke Snider, Mickey Mantle, and Mays replenished the stock as heros like Joe DiMaggio hung up their spikes.

But most of these blessings had their downside. Opening the game to African Americans was indubitably right, but it killed the Negro Leagues, ruining owners and abruptly ending many playing careers. The increasing organization of youth baseball, particularly the rise of Little League, heightened the stress of the game at its formative levels and drained much of the fun, as driven parents began to see their Junior as tomorrow's big leaguer, not as just a boy having fun while learning a thing or two. The game on the field was dominated by the home run, making for a brand of ball that some might term dull. League champs registered such stolen-base totals as Dom DiMaggio's 15 or Jackie Jensen's 22; Early Wynn led the AL in ERA one year with a mark of 3.20; and the three-base hit, despite the big old parks still prevalent, went the way of the dodo. And the pennant domination by the three New York teams—principally the Yankees, of course—made the national pastime a rather parochial pleasure; it was hard for fans in Pittsburg or Detroit to wax rhapsodic over a Subway Series. No, the blessings of the 1950s were not unmitigated, any more than on the national scene the tranquility of the Eisenhower years was without cost.

Take television, for instance: the revenues were great, and so was the publicity value of electronically extending major league play to people in southern and western areas. But the novelty of big-time heroes on the small screen kept those folks at home when formerly they had gone to the local ballpark. The minors began their long decline, one that didn't bottom out until 1964; by then the 59 leagues of 1951 had become 19, and the 8,000-odd professional players had dwindled to fewer than 2,500.

Moreover, television whetted the baseball appetites of Californians and Texans (and Georgians and Washingtonians and more). That demand plus the development of faster passenger planes gave ideas to owners of two of baseball's decaying franchises. Walter O'Mally, owner of the Brooklyn Dodgers, and Giants' owner Horace Stoneham had seen the solidarity of the original sixteen-city composition broken in 1953, when the venerable

Boston Braves (a franchise established in the first year of the National Association, 1871) became the darlings of Milwaukee, and further weakened by the defections in 1954–55 of the St. Louis Browns to Baltimore and the Philadelphia Athletics to Kansas City. Amid weeping and gnashing of teeth that continue to this day, the Dodgers and Giants left for the Golden West in 1958.

In a strange twist, the architect of the move, Walter O'Malley, was (and in the East, still is) widely reviled as the man responsible for ending the grand old game's paradisical age. Yet the placement of franchises in California, as distressing as it was for Brooklyn and Manhattan and as roundly condemned as it was by traditionalists, may now be seen as the best thing to happen to baseball in the decade. And Walter O'Malley, if you will permit your mind a considerable stretch, may be viewed not as the snake offering baseball the mortal apple but as a latter-day Johnny Appleseed (in the footsteps of Alexander Cartwright, who in 1849 also headed for California in pursuit of gold, yet who is remembered not for his venality but for bringing the New York Game to the West).

It was imperative that baseball take the game to where the people were, precisely as it had in 1903. America's population had already begun the westward and south-ward shift that was to become so pronounced in the 1960s and '70s. The move to Los Angeles and San Francisco, rather than confirming those cities' stature as "big-league," as is so often written, brought baseball into step with America, which had long recognized them as such. Baseball could now call itself the national pastime without apology.

The Sixties

A chaotic decade for our country, the 1960s were worrisome, stormy years for baseball as well, with dramatic changes in league composition, playing styles, competitive balance and, most distressingly, the game's appeal to the American people. Baseball endured its ordeal by fire, and came through not unscathed but strengthened.

The department of the Dodgers and Giants in 1958 created a vacuum in New York and an increased hunger for baseball in new boomtowns like Houston, Atlanta, and Minneapolis. Enter Branch Rickey, nearly eighty but still possessed of a keen nose for new opportunity. The great innovator who had already brought baseball the farm system and integration now created the Continental League, a paper league with paper franchises. Nonetheless, Rickey's mirage worried Organized Baseball into expansion.

Two of the Continental "franchises"—the future New

York Mets and Houston Colt .45s—were admitted for 1962. The American League was authorized to commence its western foray one year earlier with the expansion-draft Los Angeles Angels and the relocated Minnesota Twins (the latter being the transplanted Washington Senators, who were replaced in the nation's capital by an ill-fated expansion team).

Other franchise shifts and startups in the decade saw baseball's original vagabonds, the Milwaukee Braves by way of Boston, move to Atlanta in 1966. Two years later the erstwhile Athletics of Philadelphia, having failed in Kansas City, directed their caravan toward Oakland.

The A's were quickly replaced in KC by the Royals, one of two new teams introduced in each league with the expansion of 1969. This in turn precipitated divisional play and the League Championship Series, both inventions much decried at the time but now generally applauded. And in one of baseball's more forgettable debacles, the expansion Pilots of 1969 lost their course in Seattle after only one year and ran aground in Milwaukee, where they were rechristened the Brewers. The National League's expansion into San Diego and Montreal proceeded more smoothly, although Padres' attendance lagged behind expectations and the Expos' Olympic Stadium (replacing the stopgap Jarry Park) took longer to open its dome than Michelangelo took to paint St. Peter's.

On the field, the big-bang game of the 1950s was giving way to a pitching-and-defense formula, at least in the National League, which began to outstrip its longtime tormentor at the box office and in World Series and All Star confrontations. Speed returned to the equation, too, as personified by first Maury Wills and then Lou Brock (though both were preceded, in the AL, by Luis Aparicio). And a revolution in baseball strategy was brewing, as the 1959 success of such relievers as Larry Sherry, Lindy McDaniel, and Roy Face paved the way for the universal adoption of the bullpen stopper in the 1960s.

In the American League expansion year of 1961, the first played to a 162-game schedule, the Bronx Bombers hit a whopping 240 homers. Sluggers Harmon Killebrew, Norm Cash, and Rocky Colavito all hit more than 40 homers; Mickey Mantle hit more than 50. These totals were troubling to Commissioner Ford Frick, but nowhere near as consternating as the 61 homers struck by

Roger Maris to top the game's most famous record, the 60 that Babe Ruth had walloped in 1927. After seeing the National League's scoring increase in 1962, its first year of expansion, Frick became concerned that pitchers were becoming an endangered species. He said:

> I would even like the spitball to come back. Take a look at the batting, home run, and slugging record for recent seasons, and you become convinced that the pitchers need help urgently.

Disastrously, Frick convinced the owners to widen the strike zone for 1963 to its pre-1950 dimensions: top of the armpit to bottom of the knee. The result was to increase strikeouts, reduce walks, and shrink batting averages within five years to levels unseen since 1908, the nadir of the deadball era. The once-proud Yankees, who had continued their long domination of the American League to mid-decade, saw their team batting average sink to an incredible .214 in 1968. That year produced an overall AL mark of .230 and a batting champion, Carl Yastrzemski, with an average of .301.

As pitchers vanquished batters, seemingly for all eternity, the bottom line was that the fans stayed away in droves. Attendance in the National League, which in 1966 reached 15 million, fell by 1968 to only 11.7 million. In fact, despite the addition of four new clubs in 1961-62, attendance in 1968 was only 3 million more than it had been in 1960. Critics charged that baseball was a geriatric vestige of an America that had vanished, a game too slow for a nation that was rushing toward the moon; its decline would only steepen, they claimed, as that more with-it national pastime, pro football, extended its mastery of the airwaves.

But the sky was not falling, despite the alarms. The owners acted quickly to redress the game's balance between offense and defense, reducing the strike zone and lowering the pitcher's mound. But the most important change may have been one that was introduced in 1965 and was only beginning to take effect: the amateur free-agent draft. Typically, successful teams like the Yankees, Dodgers, Braves, and Cardinals had stayed successful because of their attention to scouting. Consistently they were able to garner more top prospects for their farm systems than clubs with less deep pockets or more volatile management. Now, teams that had fallen on hard times needed not look toward a generation of famine before returning to the feast. Now, dynasties—awe-inspiring but not healthy for the game—were suddenly rendered implausible. Now, baseball had a competitive balance that could produce a rotation of electrifying successes among the leagues' cities, like the ascension of the Boston Red Sox from ninth place in 1966 to the pennant the next, and the amazing rise of the New York Mets from the netherworld they had known to World Champions in 1969. The game would still have some hard rows to hoe in the 1970s, but there was no mistaking the reversal of its downturn: in the new age of "relevance," baseball was back.

The Seventies

The 1970s saw a continuation of the trend toward new stadium construction that had marked the 1960s and may well have triggered that decade's batting drought, as hitter's havens like Ebbets Field, the Polo Grounds, and Sportsman's Park fell to the wrecker's ball. The 1960s had brought new ballparks to nine cities—San Francisco, Los Angeles, New York (NL), Houston, Atlanta, Anaheim, St. Louis, Oakland, and San Diego. In 1970–71, baseball bade farewell to old friends Crosley Field, Forbes Field, and Shibe Park as new stadiums—artificial-turf clones of each other—sprang up in Cincinnati, Pittsburgh, and Philadelphia. Other new parks were built in Arlington, Kansas City, Montreal, Seattle, and Toronto (the latter two expansion franchises added to the American League in 1977), and Yankee Stadium underwent a massive facelift.

All this construction activity seemed to bespeak the

game's profitability. Indeed, attendance was climbing in almost all major league cities, as heroes like Henry Aaron, Johnny Bench, Reggie Jackson, and Pete Rose, to name but a few, gave the fans plenty to cheer about. And the controversial adoption of the designated hitter innovation by the American League in 1973 gave a further boost to hitting while giving fans much to argue about, which after all is one of the game's great pleasures.

But the game's financial health was imperiled by rising unrest over labor issues, centered on the reserve clause which bound a player to his team in perpetuity while denying him the opportunity to gauge his worth in the free market. The reformulation of the relationship between players and management became the hallmark of the decade and sorely tested fans' devotion to the game.

It began with the momentous case brought against Organized Baseball by veteran outfielder Curt Flood in 1970, challenging the legality of the reserve clause. The Supreme Court ruled against Flood the following year, but the tenor for the 1970s had been set. A thirteen-day player strike delayed the opening of the 1972 season, and arbitrator Peter Seitz ruled in 1975 (in what has come to be known as the Messersmith-McNally case) that a player could establish his right of free agency by playing out his option year without a signed contract. The writing on the wall was clear: free agency was the wave of the future.

Big-name players like Jim Hunter, Reggie Jackson, and Rich Gossage migrated to New York and lesser lights like Wayne Garland and Oscar Gamble signed elsewhere for figures that seemed incredible. In the race to sign available talent some owners spun out of control while others like Minnesota's Cal Griffith, without corporate coffers behind them, had no choice but to sit on the sidelines. Player movement among stars jeopardized fan allegiances, pundits alleged, as Gossage and Jackson played for three teams in three years and championship teams like the Oakland A's and Boston Red Sox were broken up through trades that were forced by the specter of impending—and uncompensated—free-agent departures.

(Comfortingly to the historian, all this hubbub had occurred in very much the same way in 1869–70, before the advent of the reserve clause, when Henry Chadwick was fulminating about the perniciousness of players "revolving" from one team to another simply to advance their fortunes. Also, baseball's first avowedly professional team, Harry Wright's Cincinnati Red Stockings of 1869–70, were roundly abused for constructing their powerhouse team with "mercenaries" from other states—thus scorning baseball's core appeal to civic pride.)

What actually compromised fan loyalties in the '70s was not player movement—it took Yankee fans, oh, maybe, ten minutes to regard Reggie as a born pinstriper—but player salaries. When the major-league minimum was under $5,000 or so and only a Mantle, Williams, Musial, and DiMaggio made $100,000 a year, fans saw their heroes as, by and large, working colleagues who had the supreme good fortune to play ball for a living. If a star made a splendiferous salary, that was socially useful as proof that any worker could make it big if only he had sufficient ability to emerge from the pack. But when stars began routinely to command seven-figure salaries and, more importantly, the annual wage of the average major leaguer rose to six-figure levels, and eventually seven figures, many adult breadwinners struggled to remain fans.

That they succeeded is testament to their love of the game, for fans have had a difficult assignment in reshaping their views of baseball players along the lines of media stars. The princely compensations of actors and pop musicians have long been accepted by the public as the verdict of the marketplace. If the movie *The Terminator* makes hundreds of millions of dollars for its studio and distributor, then Arnold Schwarzenegger's multimillion-dollar fee for the film seems not out of line. Analogously, if the Dodgers were fabulously lucrative for ownership, then a lofty salary for Steve Garvey ought not to have given rise in the 1970s to resentment among the fans. This sort of reeducation is by no means complete, but barroom banter about baseball by, say, 1994, was not as bitterly one-note about "greedy players" as it had been fifteen years ago.

And one didn't hear a peep about pro football replacing baseball as the national game.

The Eighties and Nineties

The game on the field in the 1970s had been marked by an unprecedented commingling of power and speed; the great teams of Cincinnati, Baltimore, and Oakland; the return to prominence of the Yankees; and the historic exploits of Henry Aaron and Pete Rose. The game in the '80s would begin with the Philadelphia Phillies, led by free-agent Rose and future Hall of Famers Mike Schmidt and Steve Carlton, ridding themselves of a historic stain. Until their victory over the Kansas City Royals, the Phils were the only one of the original sixteen major-league franchises never to have won a World Series (the St. Louis Browns had to accept the help of their modern incarnation, the Baltimore Orioles).

The next year brought baseball's darkest moment since the Brotherhood revolt and ensuing Players League of 1890, as major-league players walked off their jobs at the height of the season and didn't return for fifty days. By that time even diehard fans were thoroughly fed up with baseball's seeming inability to resolve its problems fairly and with dispatch. Talk of a fan boycott never amounted to much, but as players and management looked toward their Basic Agreement negotiation in 1989—the centenary of the Brotherhood's break with Organized Baseball—both reflected back on the damage wrought in 1981.

The 1980s brought unprecedented parity on the playing field and misery off it. The drug problem endemic in our society struck baseball inevitably as well, and Pete Rose's itch for gambling disgraced him and the game. Baseball's victims are highly publicized and their fall from grace is judged more reprehensible for all the advantages that today's players enjoy—but the game is an American institution reflecting what is wrong with our people as well as what is right with them. Let's hope that in this most difficult area of addictive behavior baseball can again—as it did with integration—lead America rather than follow it.

The year of 1989 became a nightmare, with Commissioner Bart Giamatti's expulsion of Rose followed by his own sudden and shocking death days later, a second finding of collusion by owners to undermine the free-agent market, and a Bay Area World Series rudely interrupted by an earthquake. But baseball recovered even from these calamities, as well as a spring training lockout in 1990, to embark upon an era that gave promise of unprecedented prosperity. The attendance of the Toronto Blue Jays exceeded the 4 million mark while the team captured back-to-back World Series, the first such feat since the Cincinnati Reds of 1975–1976. And in 1993 the National League expanded to fourteen teams, welcoming franchises in Miami and Colorado that were instantly and wildly prosperous, with the Rockies setting an all-time attendance peak of nearly 4.5 million fans.

And then came 1994, a year of wonderment on the playing fields, as Ken Griffey, Jr., Matt Williams, Frank Thomas, Jeff Bagwell, Tony Gwynn, Greg Maddux and a host of others appeared to be initiating a new golden age of baseball . . . until play stopped on August 12 and did not resume. The leagues, which had divided into three divisions for the first time, now had no opportunity to try out their new idea of an additional round of postseason play, with the introduction of a wild-card team that had not been a division winner.

As fans, do we side with the players, who went on strike hoping to extend their gains of the previous two decades? Or do we side with the owners, who stood fast in insisting upon a balance between costs and revenues? As fans, we would do well to side with the game of baseball, and wish that its most intense contests reconvene to the field of play.

Baseball is not a conventional industry. It belongs neither to the players nor management, but to all of us. It is our national pastime, our national symbol, and our national treasure.

Each of us has deplored the present state of things, and has thought back to his personal version of the good old days. But make no mistake about it—our game, the American game, will become stronger than before for having passed through its crucible of 1994.

The Weather of Our Lives

Ever changing in ways that are so small as to preserve the illusion that "nothing changes in baseball," the game has introduced, in the lifetime of many of us: night ball, plane travel, television, integration, bullpen stoppers, expansion, the amateur draft, competitive parity, indoor stadiums, artificial turf, free agency, the designated hitter, and international play. Not far off, perhaps, are further expansions to thirty-two teams, interleague contests, and intercontinental championships.

For fans accustomed to the game's languorous rhythms and conservative resistance to innovation, the changes of the past twenty years in particular seem positively frenetic. Yet for all its changes, baseball has not strayed far from its origins, and in fact has changed far less than other American institutions of equivalent antiquity. What sustains baseball in the hearts of Americans, finally, is not its responsiveness to changes in society nor its propensity for novelty, but its myths, its lore, its records, and its essential stability. As historian Bruce Catton noted in 1959:

> A gaffer from the era of William McKinley, abruptly brought back to the second half of the twentieth century, would find very little in modern life that would not seem new, strange, and rather bewildering, but put in a good grandstand seat back of first base he would see nothing that was not completely familiar.

It's still a game of bat and ball, played without regard for the clock; a game of ninety-foot basepaths, nine innings, nine men in the field; three outs, all out; and three strikes still send you to the bench, no matter whom you know in city hall. It's the national anthem before every game; it's playing catch with your son or daughter; it's learning how to win and how to deal with loss, and how to connect with something larger than ourselves.

"Baseball," wrote Thomas Wolfe, "has been not merely 'the great national game' but really a part of the whole weather of our lives, of the thing that is our own,

of the whole fabric, the million memories of America."
Spring comes in America not on the vernal equinox but
on opening day; summer sets in with a Memorial Day
doubleheader and does not truly end until the last out of
the regular season. Winter begins the day after the
World Series.

Where were you when Bobby Thomson hit the shot
heard 'round the world? Or the night Carlton Fisk hit
his homer in the twelfth? Or when the Mets, with batter
after batter one strike away from their loss in the World
Series, staged their famous rally? These are milestones
in the lives of America and Americans.

We grow up with baseball; we mark—and, for a moment, stop—the passage of time with it; and we grow
old with it. It is our game, for all our days.

PENGUIN 60s

are published on the occasion of Penguin's 60th anniversary

FOR THE BEST IN PAPERBACKS, LOOK FOR THE

In every corner of the world, on every subject under the sun, Penguin represents quality and variety—the very best in publishing today.

For complete information about books available from Penguin—including Puffins, Penguin Classics, and Arkana—and how to order them, write to us at the appropriate address below. Please note that for copyright reasons the selection of books varies from country to country.

In the United States: Please write to *Consumer Sales, Penguin USA, P.O. Box 999, Dept. 17109, Bergenfield, New Jersey 07621-0120.* VISA and MasterCard holders call 1-800-253-6476 to order all Penguin titles.

In Canada: Please write to *Penguin Books Canada Ltd, 10 Alcorn Avenue, Suite 300, Toronto, Ontario M4V 3B2.*

In the United Kingdom: Please write to *Dept. JC, Penguin Books Ltd, FREEPOST, West Drayton, Middlesex UB7 OBR.*